Dear Parent:
Your child's love of re

Every child learns to read in a diffε speed. Some go back and forth between reading levels and read favorite books again and again. Others read through each level in order. You can help your young reader improve and become more confident by encouraging his or her own interests and abilities. From books your child reads with you to the first books he or she reads alone, there are I Can Read Books for every stage of reading:

SHARED READING
Basic language, word repetition, and whimsical illustrations, ideal for sharing with your emergent reader

BEGINNING READING
Short sentences, familiar words, and simple concepts for children eager to read on their own

READING WITH HELP
Engaging stories, longer sentences, and language play for developing readers

READING ALONE
Complex plots, challenging vocabulary, and high-interest topics for the independent reader

I Can Read Books have introduced children to the joy of reading since 1957. Featuring award-winning authors and illustrators and a fabulous cast of beloved characters, I Can Read Books set the standard for beginning readers.

A lifetime of discovery begins with the magical words **"I Can Read!"**

Visit www.icanread.com for information
on enriching your child's reading experience.

I Can Read® and I Can Read Book® are trademarks of HarperCollins Publishers.

Love, Diana: Meet Diana
TM & © 2022 PocketWatch, Inc. & PocketAction, LLC.
All Rights Reserved. Love, Diana and all related titles, logos and characters, and the
pocket.watch logo are trademarks of PocketWatch, Inc. All other rights are the property
of their respective owners. Printed in the United States of America.
No part of this book may be used or reproduced in any manner whatsoever without written permission except
in the case of brief quotations embodied in critical articles and reviews. For information address
HarperCollins Children's Books, a division of HarperCollins Publishers, 195 Broadway, New York, NY 10007.
www.icanread.com

Library of Congress Control Number: 2021942273
ISBN 978-0-06-320439-3

21 22 23 24 25 LSCC 10 9 8 7 6 5 4 3 2 1 ❖ First Edition

I Can Read!

1 BEGINNING READING

pocket.watch™

Love, Diana™

Meet Diana

HARPER
An Imprint of HarperCollinsPublishers

Meet Diana!

She believes that everyone

can be who they want to be.

They just need to believe it!

When Diana uses her imagination,
she is the Princess of Play.

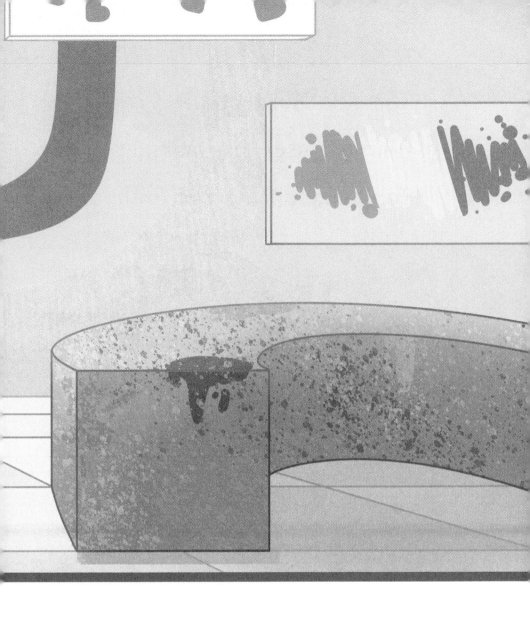

She loves dressing up.

Diana can be anyone she wants to be.

Roma is Diana's brother.

When he uses his imagination,

Roma is the Prince of Pretend.

Roma loves to play with his sister.

But sometimes he can get

them into trouble.

Oh, Roma!

Mama and Papa are their parents.
They tell Diana and Roma they
can be whoever they want to be.

If you play it, you can be it!

Diana loves her family.

They make playtime even more fun!

Diana and Roma go on adventures
in the Land of Play!

This is a world full of magical
creatures and animal friends.

This is Winston.

Winston is Diana's dog.

He is the cutest!

When Winston loses his bone in the
Land of Play, Diana helps him find it.

Bonnie the Bunny loves to bake.

But sometimes her recipes

don't work out.

In the Land of Play,

Diana and Roma become chefs

and fix Bonnie's kitchen troubles.

Looks yummy!

Then there is Honey.

She is a beautiful horse.

She has wings, a crown,

and a bow on her tail.

When she has a hair emergency,

Diana and Roma head to the salon.

Honey looks cute in no time!

Speaking of cute,

this is Koko the Kittycorn.

She has a rainbow horn and tail.

When the evil Boris ruins
Kittycorn's scratching post,
artists Diana and Roma help her.
They even bring along
their own cat.

Diana protects her friends from boredom in the Land of Play.

Boris is the Baron of Boredom.

He is the most boring villain of all!

Boris and his minions hate fun and joy.

They will stop at nothing

to ruin everyone's fun.

All of Diana's

sweet friends

make Boris mad.

Boris absolutely hates fun!

Diana tries to be nice to Boris.

She gives him a card.

See, Boris?

Hearts and fun always save the day.

Luckily, Diana has lots of magical

ways to keep the fun going.

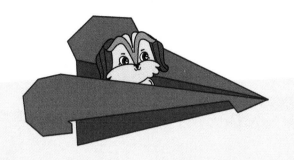

Diana even has a Bubble Mobile

to fly around the Land of Play!

Inside her Backpack,

Diana keeps her favorite

accessories with her.

Her hairbrush has

a magic Playstone inside of it.

And her ribbons light up when

boredom is brewing!

Diana's Magic Trunk

has all the costumes she needs.

Diana can be a singer, a scuba diver,

a scientist, and so much more!

When you play pretend,

you can be anything you dream.

Just like Diana!

Another **Love, Diana** book for you to love:

Visit **ICanRead.com** for
a complete list of **I Can Read** books,
as well as tips for parents and educators!

I Can Read!

BEGINNING READING 1

Meet Diana and her adorable family and friends.

My First — Ideal for sharing with emergent readers

1 — Short sentences, familiar words, and simple concepts for children eager to read on their own

2 — Engaging stories for developing readers

3 — Complex plots for confident readers

GUIDED READING LEVEL **J**

HARPER
An Imprint of HarperCollins*Publishers*
ICanRead.com

TM & © 2022 PocketWatch, Inc.
All Rights Reserved.

An **I Can Read Book**